BEAR'S BUSY FAMILY

Written by Stella Blackstone
Illustrated by Debbie Harter

Smell the bread
my grandma bakes

Touch the bowls
my grandpa makes

Taste the fish
my uncle brings

Hear the songs
my auntie sings

See the dress
my mummy sews

Smell the flowers
my daddy grows

**Touch the plums
my sister picks**

Taste the bowl
my brother licks

Hear the drums
my cousins play

See the feast for baby's birthday!

My Family Tree

grandma

daddy

baby

mummy

sister

brother

me

grandpa

uncle

auntie

cousins

For Mo, Kirsten, Matthew, Alice and Chloë — D.H.
For the Luecks, who are a very busy family — S.B.

Barefoot Beginners
an imprint of
Barefoot Books
124 Walcot Street
Bath
BA1 5BG

Graphic design by Amesbury Grzelinski Ltd., Bath
Colour separation by Grafiscan, Verona
Printed and bound in Singapore by Tien Wah Press (Pte) Ltd.

This book was typeset in Futura and illustrated in watercolour,
pen and ink and crayon on thick watercolour paper

This book has been printed on 100% acid-free paper

Hardback ISBN 1 902283 89 9
Paperback ISBN 1 902283 91 0

British Cataloguing-in-Publication Data: a catalogue record for this
book is available from the British Library

3 5 7 9 8 6 4 2